Toe Beans

From The Series
Lee Lee's Big Adventures

There should be no "hush" about those things that
make us different.

To Charlie

Story & Concept by Steven Foreman

Illustrated by Kristen Leigh Brown

My name is Lee Lee. I can do many things with the five little, squishy, black toe beans on my one front leg. I use them like you use your fingers. Can you count them?

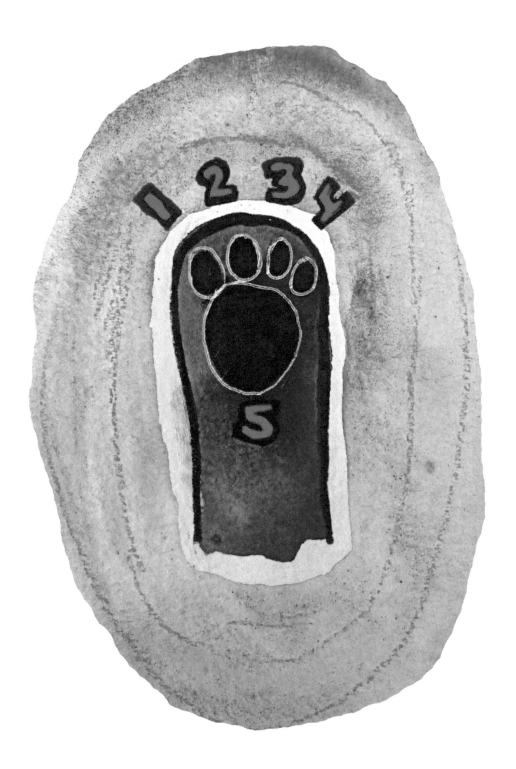

I am so tall! I can stretch myself up the walls and turn on the light switches in my house with my toe beans! It is very funny. Have you ever seen a cat turn on a light switch?

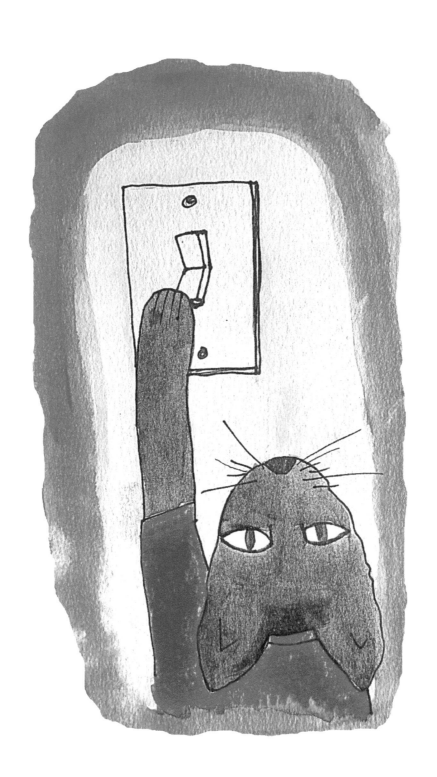

I can get ice cubes from the big refrigerator with my toe beans. I hit them around on the floor. When I go back to play with them, there is just water there. I lick it up. Where did the ice cubes go?

I like bags and purses. When people aren't looking, I get inside and touch their things with my toe beans. I have to be very quiet so they don't hear me or else they will say, "No, Lee Lee!"

**Look at all the
treasures I find!**

One time I found a little bottle of paint in a bag, and I had lots of fun with it. I chewed the lid off and stamped my toe beans all over the place. Have you ever made a mess?

When I do something bad, I just make myself look really cute. I lay with my toe beans on a toy. I look at my people until they just can't stand to be mad at me anymore.

**My stuffed mouse is
my favorite toy!**

Last week I ate at the salad bar and knocked it over with my toe beans. My people call it a houseplant. I have eaten a few of them. They always just get a new one.

Yum! I like what is
on the menu today!

I have a girlfriend who comes to my house to visit. I don't go outside very much, because I don't like to get my toe beans dirty. She doesn't seem to mind dirty toe beans.

**Isn't she pretty? I
like her very much.**

I like to watch videos of birds and squirrels. I watch them for hours. Sometimes I try to lift the computer up with my toe beans or look behind it to see where they go. Where do they go?

I like birds the most!

I like to sneak off and play in the water in the kitchen or the bathroom. I hit it with my toe beans and it splashes everywhere. Then I stick my tongue in and get a drink.

I like to lay on my people's books and dream about what the story might be inside. I rub my toe beans on the book and let my kitty imagination run wild.

I like books. Do you
like books?

I dream about my many adventures. I can do so many things and all of them make me happy to just be me. I like the way I am, and I like the way you are. We are very special.

**Goodnight.
You are my special
friend.**

CPSIA information can be obtained
at www.ICGtesting.com
Printed in the USA
LVHW072130070319
609934LV00026B/596/P